Hafsa
and the
Magical Ring

by Yasmin Ullah

Illustrated by Rafiuzzaman Rhythom

To my mother, my younger self, and to Rohingya children everywhere;
may your future, hopes and dreams grow beautifully.
- Yasmin Ullah

This is for Ammu, Abbu and Tulipu. Thank you for the love and support.
- Rafiuzzaman Rhythom

Text copyright © 2022 by Yasmin Ullah
Illustrations copyright © 2022 by Rafiuzzaman Rhythom

ISBN (English hardcover edition) 978-1-946747-24-2
ISBN (Bangla hardcover edition) 978-1-946747-25-9

Bangla translation by Qazi Shamim Hasan

Edited by Raya Rahman
Cover design by Rafiuzzaman Rhythom
Book layout by Inshra Sakhawat Russell, Studio Inku

This book was typeset in Oldenburg
The illustrations for this book were created digitally

First Edition

Guba Publishing LLC
2323 Broadway
Oakland, California 94612

Visit us at www.gubabooks.com

From the doorway of her shelter, Hafsa watched the clouds go by. They made pretty shapes in the sky, like floating cotton balls. How nice it would be to touch one!

"Vroom, vroom!" Her little brother, Hafiz, was playing a few steps away. "Stay close to the shelter," Hafsa reminded him. She didn't want him to wander off and get lost.

They lived with their mother in a very big refugee camp. Even after a few years, Hafsa was still not used to the place.

She missed the lush green trees and the mountains of her homeland. And her family and friends who were no longer with them.

Still, they had made new friends at the camp.
The kind lady from a nearby shelter sometimes
shared fish she bought at the market.

And that day would be like Eid! Hafsa thought
her mother was the best cook in the world.
Most days they ate rice and lentils. But Mama
managed to make this simple dish taste special
each time.

When lunch was ready, Hafsa called her brother to come inside. But Hafiz just stood there with a cheeky smile. What was he hiding behind his back?

She shook his hands until an old razor fell to the ground. Hafsa was shocked. "This is so dangerous! We have to go see Mama," she said, rushing him inside.

Luckily, the blade was dull, and Hafiz did not cut himself. Mama made sure that he washed his hands with soap to be extra safe. "A razor is not a toy, Hafiz," she gently scolded.

For some reason, her mother's words filled Hafsa with strange emotions. Before she could help it, tears were rolling down her face.

"What's wrong, lalabi?" Mama asked. Hafsa loved being called lalabi. It meant 'most beautiful' in her language. "Don't worry, Hafiz is not hurt!" her mother assured her.

Mama worked hard to care for them, so Hafsa always tried to be cheery around her. But this time, she didn't hide her feelings. She couldn't bear to see her little brother playing with a dangerous object. "I wish I could give Hafiz my old toys," she whispered.

A gentle, weary smile spread across Mama's face.

"What old toys?" she asked. "You know- the glasses and watches you used to make for me." Hafsa's face lit up as she remembered.

"Especially the rings!"

"Mama, you made toys?" Hafiz was very impressed. He wondered what other fantastic things his mother could do.

"That's right, Hafiz," Hafsa explained. "Mama made the most beautiful toys from screw-pine leaves!"
"What's screw-pine?" he asked.

"Screw-pine was nature's gift to us," Mama answered. "It was abundant in our homeland. Our elders taught us how to make mats, containers and many other useful things with them."

"And toys too!" Hafsa exclaimed.

"Tell me more!" Hafiz shouted gleefully. "Did Baba also make things from screwpine leaves?"

Mama and Hafsa exchanged glances. It was not easy for Hafsa to talk about her late father.

But she wanted her brother to know him like she did. "Baba was the one who cut the leaves," she said proudly. "First, he'd get rid of all the prickly parts. Then he would soak and dry them in the sun, ready for Mama and Dadi to make wonderful things with."

"What was Dadi like?" Hafiz asked. He was little when they left home, so he didn't remember their grandmother.

"Dadi was a skilled weaver," Hafsa recalled. "All the aunties in our village would gather in our yard to learn her techniques."

Mama laughed and said, "She always joked that she had magical hands."

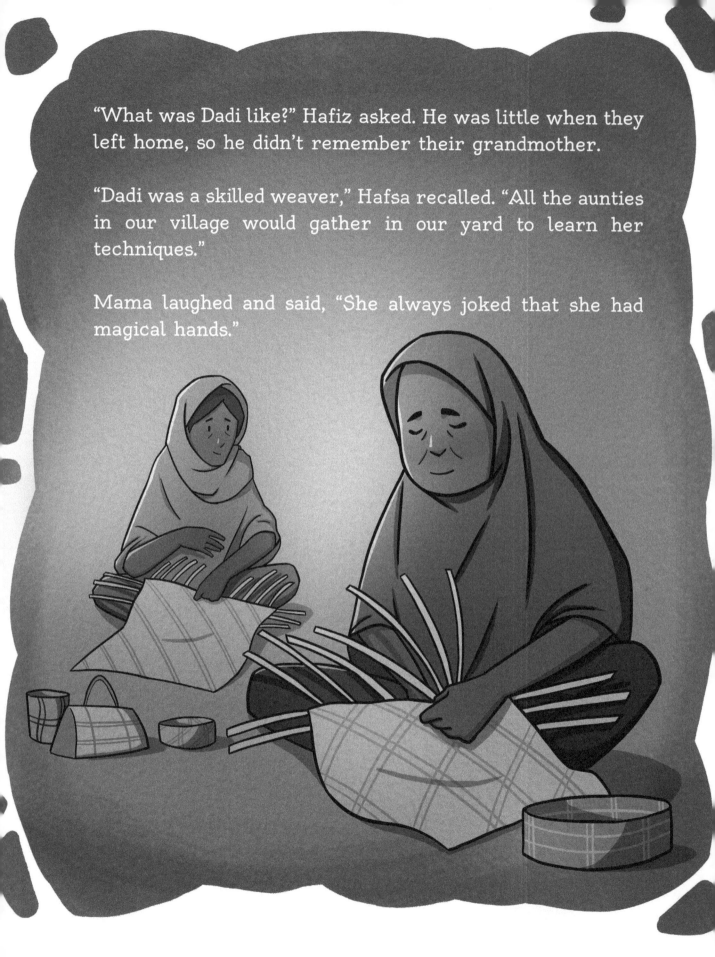

"Dadi was also the life of the party!" Hafsa giggled. She always wondered if people came to learn weaving or to hear her grandmother's stories. Maybe both, she thought.

"I wish I could hear her stories one more time," Hafsa sighed.

"Story! Story!" Hafiz jumped up and down. "Mama, do you know any stories?"

Once again, a gentle, weary smile spread on Mama's face. "Dadi used to tell Hafsa this folktale at bedtime. I'll try my best to tell it like her."

Once upon a time, there was a king who ruled a prosperous kingdom with the help of a magical ring that could grant wishes. The only condition was that he needed to take care of the ring.

But the king was careless! While crossing a river on his horse, he dropped it in the water by mistake. The king fell into despair and commanded all his servants to look for his magical ring. But no one could find it.

One day, a poor farmer's son went to buy fish in the market. He bought the smallest fish as that was all he could afford. When his widowed mother was about to cook it, she found a beautiful golden ring inside.

Excited and grateful, they kept the ring a secret and took great care of it. Then one night, the ring spoke, and asked if the farmer's son had any wishes.

He wished for a new house and enough wealth, so they didn't go hungry anymore. Eventually, the boy started to take care of those less fortunate. He wished to build schools and wells, and to grow enough food to feed the poor people in his village.

Soon, his generosity became well known far and wide. Another king heard of his kind heart, and asked him to marry the king's daughter. The farmer's son married the princess and they lived happily ever after.

Hafiz's eyes were filled with wonder. "What happened to the ring, Mama?" he asked.

"It disappeared," she said mysteriously. "But it may reappear again, if it finds a rightful owner who is gentle, kind and honest. Like the farmer's son."

Hafsa knew it was just a story, but she wished she found the king's magical ring. She would use it to turn things back to the way they were.

"Mama, do you think I am honest and kind?" Hafsa asked quietly.

"There is no other like you, my love," said her mother.

The next day, Mama had a surprise for them. With
the help of their friends at the camp, she managed to
collect some bright pieces of paper. Hafiz got a smart
looking paper watch, handmade by Mama.

For Hafsa, Mama made a ring. "I'm sorry it's not magical," she said.

"No, Mama! It's beautiful!" Hafsa exclaimed.

"Just like you, lalabi," her mother whispered.

Gom Acho Collection

 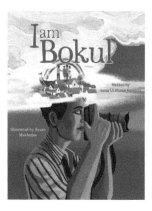  

Afterword

Gom acho is a common greeting used by both Rohingyas and Bangladeshis in Cox's Bazar to ask, How are you? This story is part of our Gom Acho Collection that represents and affirms the lives of children affected by the refugee experience. The stories are intended to bring enjoyment to all children and foster increased learning, confidence, and social cohesion.

To create this collection, the Asia Foundation and Guba Books benefitted from the input of youth living in and near refugee settlements in Cox's Bazar, Bangladesh.

Author: Yasmin Ullah
Yasmin Ullah is a Rohingya human rights activist. She was born in the Northern Rakhine state of Myanmar. She published her poetry in the Anthology: I Am A Rohingya in 2019, and later in 2021, she was named on the FemiList100, the Gender Security Project list of 100 women from the Global South, working in foreign policy, peacebuilding, law, activism, and development.

Twitter: @YasminJUllah

Illustrator: Rafiuzzaman Rhythom
Rafiuzzaman Rhythom is a Bangladeshi illustrator and animator. From a very young age he was drawn towards cartoons and comics and wanted to become an artist. After getting his BFA and MFA degrees from Faculty of Fine Art, University of Dhaka, he is now living his childhood dreams. He worked in Bangladesh's first 2D animated feature film "Mujib Amar Pita" as a character designer and animator.

Instagram: @rhythom.with.an.o

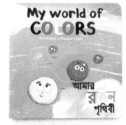

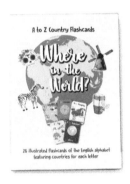

Don't miss our other titles!
Simply visit www.gubabooks.com

gubabooks